A Time to Dance

Virginia's Civil War Diary
Book Three

by Mary Pope Osborne
and Will Osborne

Scholastic Inc. New York

New York City
1865

July 2, 1865

At last we are settled in our new home in New York City.

Pa, Jane Ellen, Abraham Lincoln Dickens, and I arrived last night. Baby Abe slept in his little basket for most of the trip, covered with a red blanket. When Jed helped us carry him off the train, he said we looked as if we were headed for a picnic!

I think I am going to love our life here. I already love the home Jed has found for us — a small set of furnished rooms above Brown's Shoe Store on Third Street. Jed and Jane Ellen will take the large front room, with Baby Abe in a cradle next to their bed. Pa will sleep in the small bedroom. I will have a cot in a room off the kitchen that was once the pantry.

I think our rooms here are much nicer than our rooms in Washington City. The front room even has a piano! And Jane Ellen knows how to play!

Now it is early morning, and she is playing a soft, happy tune. Carriages rattle by on the street outside. A woman strolls down the sidewalk with a basket on her head, calling, "Strawberries! Fresh strawberries!"

New York seems a bit like a picnic indeed.

July 3, 1865

I have spent all morning cleaning our new home. Jane Ellen helped for a while, but quickly became too exhausted. She has not fully regained her strength since Baby Abe was born. The two of them are sleeping now. They both look quite pale and fragile.

Pa is practicing his violin in his room. This afternoon he will set out to look for work. He has a letter from Professor Withers, the conductor of the orchestra at Ford's New Theatre in Washington. The letter praises Pa's character, and his talent as a musician.

Ford's New Theatre has been closed since President Lincoln was assassinated there three months ago. Professor Withers told Pa he thought there would be more opportunity for a musician with his talent in New York.

Jed left early for his first day at his new job. He will be writing for a newspaper called the *Spirit of the Times*. The editor there offered him the job because he had read Jed's articles about life in Washington City. He said he liked the way Jed's mind worked.

The editor said that Jed would be writing

mostly about plays and sporting events. But he promised that sometimes Jed could just write what he thinks.

I love it when Jed writes what he thinks. His thoughts are brilliant. At least, that's what *I* think.

July 4, 1865

Today is Independence Day. There is to be a grand parade down Fifth Avenue. Jed is going to write about it for his newspaper.

Pa said we should all go with Jed to the parade and celebrate our country. He said that with the war finally over, Independence Day means more than ever before.

Evening

The parade was magnificent. Thousands of Union soldiers marched with their regiments. Many walked on crutches. Some had only one arm or one leg. But they all looked proud and brave. One soldier was blind. But, led by two of his fellow soldiers, he carried the American flag for his regiment.

By the end of the parade, my throat was sore from cheering and my hands were red from clapping. I wanted every single soldier to know how grateful I was for his bravery and courage.

When we got home, Jed went straight to his desk. By the time he finished writing, Jane Ellen, Pa, and Baby Abe were all asleep. Jed tapped softly on the door of my pantry room and asked if I was still awake. When I said I was, he asked if he could read his article to me.

In his article, Jed told all about the parade, and the soldiers, and the blind man carrying the flag. Here's how he ended his story:

The States of the nation are again United, and once more a single flag floats supreme over every inch of our magnificent country. The wounds of the war ache still, but the nation's heart beats strong. The country is whole and its people are free. The healing has begun.

I love what Jed wrote. But even more, I love that he wanted to share his writing with me.

July 5, 1865

Early this morning, I set out to explore. Pa had left to look for work, Jed had gone to his job at the newspaper, and Jane Ellen and Baby

Abe had fallen back asleep. I left a note for Jane Ellen, saying I had gone to the market and would be back very soon.

What I saw on my walk was amazing.

I passed houses that looked like palaces, with grand entrances and columns and lawns and beautiful tall windows.

Then, just a few blocks away, I saw filthy streets with dirty brick buildings all crammed together like rows of toy blocks.

There were beggars on almost every corner. In some places, whole families sat in the street, asking for pennies from anyone who passed by.

It is hard to believe that two such different worlds can exist in the same city. Our world seems to be somewhere in between.

I do not want us ever to be poor. Until Pa finds a job with an orchestra, I wonder if I myself should not be out looking for work.

July 7, 1865

Pa heard today that soldiers blocked the entrance to Mr. Ford's theatre in Washington City when he tried to reopen it. The government has ordered that there be no more plays there.

Jed says many people have turned against the theatre because President Lincoln's assassin, John Wilkes Booth, was an actor. This does not seem at all right to me! President Lincoln loved plays. I do not think he would want people to stop going to the theatre.

I told Jed my thoughts, and he agreed. But he said John Wilkes Booth's brother Edwin is also an actor. Many people think Edwin Booth is the greatest actor of our time. But he has sworn never to return to the stage because his brother John has disgraced his family.

Our mother was born in Virginia. She had

two brothers. They may have fought for the Confederacy. They might have even shot one of the men I saw marching in the parade on Independence Day. I wonder: Are Jed and I disgraced because our uncles were Rebs?

July 8, 1865

This morning we heard newsboys on the corner calling, "Extra! Conspirators hanged! Read all about the hanging!" I rushed out and bought one of their papers for a penny.

The paper said that the four conspirators who helped John Wilkes Booth plan President Lincoln's assassination were hanged yesterday in Washington. Hundreds of people came to watch. The article said there was a "universal feeling of satisfaction" in the city.

I find this strange. Hanging the conspirators will not bring the President back to life.

Right now, I do not have a feeling of satisfaction. I just feel very sad.

July 9, 1865

Jed had his first assignment at a theatre last night. He saw *The Widow's Victim* at the New Bowery Theatre. At breakfast he told us all about it. He said the crowd was very rowdy and the evening was very long. Now he must write what he thinks of the play for the paper.

I would love to see a play. Perhaps I can convince Jed to take me with him when he goes to the theatre again.

Later

At supper I asked Jed about going with him to see a play. He said there was very little onstage that was suitable for a young girl to see.

I said I was not so young, that I was very interested in the theatre, and that in all New York City there must surely be *something* suitable.

Jed said he would ask his new friends at the newspaper if they can think of anything.

July 11, 1865

Hooray! Jed has promised to take me to the theatre! We will spend the afternoon on Saturday at Mr. P. T. Barnum's American Museum. The museum has a menagerie of animals, exhibits of ancient curiosities from all over the world, and a grand lecture hall where plays are performed every day.

Jed brought home an advertisement for the

show that is playing there now. Here is what the advertisement says we will see:

Claude Marcel or The Idiot of Tarbes
A Grand Romantic Tragedy featuring
New and Splendid Scenic Effects, and
Appropriate Appointments and Costumes

A grand romantic tragedy! I can hardly wait.

July 12, 1865

This morning I took a walk down Broadway to see P. T. Barnum's American Museum. It is magnificent! It is five stories tall and takes up almost an entire block!

Jed says Mr. Barnum is famous for playing jokes on the public. He once advertised a "six-foot-tall man-eating chicken." When the curtain went up, there was a man onstage eating a chicken leg. He was a six-foot-tall man . . . eating chicken! Not a chicken who ate men!

People laughed, and only a few wanted their money back. Can you imagine? I hope the show on Saturday is better than that!

July 13, 1865

I cannot believe that in two days I am finally going to see a play. I was supposed to go to the theatre for the very first time the night President Lincoln was shot.

On that night, Pa was playing in the orchestra at Mr. Ford's theatre. He was going to let me stand in the back and watch a play called *Our American Cousin*. But when the newspapers announced that President Lincoln was going to attend the play that night, Pa said he would not be able to sneak me in.

I was so disappointed that I cried for hours.

I thought it was a great tragedy that I could not go to the theatre. I did not know how great the tragedy would truly be that night.

On Saturday, I will wear the lacy yellow dress Jane Ellen gave me to wear to Ford's Theatre. Before I go, I will say a prayer for President Lincoln and his family.

July 14, 1865

I will not wear my yellow dress to P. T. Barnum's American Museum tomorrow. I will not see the show there, or the menagerie, or the ancient curiosities. Why? Because Mr. Barnum's museum has burned to the ground.

Jed says firemen worked for hours to put out the fire. They saved all the people who were inside. Still, Mr. Barnum's museum was completely destroyed and most of the animals in his menagerie died in the fire.

Thousands of people turned out to watch the building burn. While the firemen worked to put out the flames, pickpockets moved through the crowd. They stole men's wallets and ladies' purses. Thieves also stole things from the stores and shops around the museum.

How can some people be so terrible?

July 15, 1865

This was the day I was to go with Jed to see the play at Mr. Barnum's museum. Instead, I spent the afternoon in bed in my little pantry room. I told Pa and Jane Ellen I felt sick. But what I truly feel is terribly, terribly sad. I keep thinking of the animals who suffered in the fire, and of the firemen risking their lives, and of the pickpockets and thieves.

I think of the sad, dirty families begging on the streets just a few blocks from our home.

I think of the blind and wounded soldiers in the parade, and of John Wilkes Booth, and the conspirators who were hanged in Washington.

And I think of President Lincoln's family, and how heartbroken they must all still be.

I no longer want to go the theatre to watch a "grand romantic tragedy." There is too much tragedy in the world already.

July 16, 1865

At breakfast this morning, Jed said he was "keeping his eye out" for another play that we could see together. I told him he needn't bother, that I had lost my interest in the theatre.

The truth is, I do not feel much interest in anything these days.

July 19, 1865

It has been very hot all week. Jane Ellen has spent most of the last few days in bed. I'm sure the weather is making her feel even more exhausted than usual. She never complains, though. She gently rocks Baby Abe's cradle beside her bed, while he frets about the heat.

Later

Pa came home this afternoon in poor spirits. He says it is a terrible time to look for work as a musician, as many theatres do not even operate in the summer. It makes me sad to picture him carrying his violin all over the city in this heat.

No one has suggested that I go to work. But I feel I should help earn money for our rent and food. We have not discussed my schooling yet. Nor have we spoken about what we will do if Pa cannot find work here as a musician. Even though we have unpacked all our belongings, our home still feels very unsettled.

July 20, 1865

I bought a newspaper this morning and looked in the Advertisements section for a job. There were many notices for girls to work in factories as trimmers or cutters. I do not know what these jobs are.

July 22, 1865

Today Jed lent me his book of plays by William Shakespeare. He said there would be many plays by Shakespeare coming to New York in the fall, and one of them would surely be suitable for us to see together.

I reminded Jed that I was no longer interested in plays and the theatre. He just smiled and handed me the book anyway.

July 24, 1865

I have been trying to read the plays of William Shakespeare. Jed says the writing is poetry. I see that some of the lines rhyme, but most do not. How can that be poetry?

July 26, 1865

Pa still has had no success finding a job with an orchestra. People tell him there will be more work for musicians when "the season" begins in September.

I told Pa not to worry. I said that I wanted to help our family, and could perhaps get a job in one of the factories.

"Nonsense!" he said. "We'll hear no more about that!"

I think I hurt his feelings. I know how frustrated he is about not being able to support his family.

July 27, 1865

This morning, Pa told us he was putting an advertisement in the paper seeking violin students. He asked Jane Ellen if he could use the front room for his lessons.

"Oh yes!" she said. She assured him that we could tend to Baby Abe in his room while he teaches out front.

Pa taught violin lessons when we lived in Gettysburg. He had hoped his teaching days were over. But now he seems resigned to going back to it.

July 29, 1865

I lay awake much of last night, thinking that Pa is not very smart about money. It will surely be a long while before he has enough violin students to earn much.

So this morning, on my way to the market, I walked quickly to the address of one of the factories I had read about in the Advertisements section of the paper. I climbed a creaky set of stairs and peered into a dim, windowless room.

What I saw was horrible. Dozens of women and girls were working at machines. Some of the girls were even younger than I. The air was stale and damp. The smell was terrible and the heat nearly unbearable. And the noise! The noise was almost deafening. I covered my ears and ran back down the stairs.

I do not know what to do. I cannot imagine

working in such a place. I could apply for a job as a servant in a wealthy person's home. But then I would not be able to help Jane Ellen take care of the baby during the day.

Why must we always be struggling? I thought our lives in New York would be different.

July 31, 1865

There was a notice in Jed's newspaper today about a contest for Civil War veterans — a left-handed penmanship contest. Any Union soldier who lost his right arm in the war may compete. The soldier with the best handwriting will receive five hundred dollars. The contest is supposed to inspire veterans to overcome their handicaps and build new lives.

As I write this, Pa is practicing his violin. Jane Ellen is playing the piano. Jed is gently rocking Baby Abe in his arms. I am ashamed of my feelings of discontent. I must try to remember how lucky we are.

August 3, 1865

We finally had a discussion about my schooling. I think Pa and Jed had been putting it off because of Jane Ellen's health. Here is what we decided: For at least another year, I will study my lessons at home with Jane Ellen. I will help her take care of Baby Abe and keep house.

I do not mind this arrangement at all. Jane Ellen is a wonderful teacher. And to be honest, I was a little afraid of what the schools here in New York would be like.

August 8, 1865

Jane Ellen got a letter from her friend Becky Lee in Gettysburg today. Becky Lee had wonderful news. She has found her mother's brother and his family, and they are coming to live with her!

Becky Lee's relatives were all slaves on a plantation in South Carolina. Becky Lee had been trying to locate them since the war ended. Finally she received word from someone who had seen one of her notices in a South Carolina newspaper.

Becky Lee traveled to a little town near Charleston and found them living in a shack on their former owner's land. She said there were seven people sharing a room the size of our parlor in Gettysburg.

August 10, 1865

I cannot stop thinking about Becky Lee's relatives. In her letter, Becky Lee said there was a girl in the family about my age. The girl must have been a slave, too.

I have tried over and over to imagine how it would feel to be *owned* by another person. But I cannot do it. I simply cannot imagine it. And I cannot imagine how anyone could ever believe it was all right to own slaves.

August 15, 1865

Pa has received no inquiries from his notice seeking students. I told him that no one can think of violin lessons in this weather. I said that as soon as the heat spell ends, people will think of music again.

August 17, 1865

Jed has found another play for us to see together. It is a play by William Shakespeare called *King Lear*. It will be performed at the Broadway Theatre on Broome Street. We will see it in two weeks.

I must admit, I am rather excited. I thought I had lost my interest in the theatre. But perhaps not.

August 19, 1865

I told Jane Ellen today that I could not understand the poetry in Jed's Shakespeare book and was worried that I would not be able to enjoy *King Lear*. She says we can use *King Lear* for our first reading lesson.

August 22, 1865

I have been trying to read *King Lear*. Jane Ellen is helping me understand the story. It is all about a king who gives his kingdom to his daughters and then goes insane when they turn against him.

August 25, 1865

Jed invited a friend from the newspaper to join us for supper tonight. During the meal, there was a lot of talk about President Johnson.

When he was Vice President, Mr. Johnson spoke very harshly about the South. But now he believes the South should be treated with leniency. He says the government should help the South recover from the war.

Many Northern congressmen, though, are

still very angry. They think the South should be punished.

I truly do not know what I think. When I think of Becky Lee and her family, and the wounded soldiers, and the assassination of President Lincoln, I, too, feel angry. But when I remember Captain Heath, the Confederate officer who saved me in Gettysburg, and his family in North Carolina, I do not want him to be punished. And when I remember that my mother's brothers may have been Confederate soldiers, I do not want them punished, either.

How is it possible to feel such different things at the same time?

August 30, 1865

Good news! Pa has received his first inquiry for music lessons! A letter arrived from a woman who said she very much wishes for her son to learn the violin. She says she is seeking a patient and talented instructor.

Pa replied immediately. He said he was eager to assist her and was certain he could teach her son to play. He said he would charge three dollars a month, and that she should bring her son for a lesson every week.

Pa seemed very happy that someone finally noticed his advertisement. I hope, I hope, I hope the woman accepts his terms.

September 4, 1865

I am still reading *King Lear*. The plot has gotten very complicated. Many people have been killed or banished.

September 6, 1865

Jed wrote an article for his paper this week about President Johnson and his enemies in Congress. Some congressmen are now saying that Jefferson Davis, the President of the Confederacy, should be hanged, like the conspirators who helped John Wilkes Booth murder President Lincoln. They say the Confederacy tried to murder the nation.

In his article, Jed said what most threatens to murder the nation now is the hatred that rages in some of its leaders. He reminded people of President Lincoln's words: "With malice toward none, with charity for all . . ."

September 11, 1865

Hooray! Pa received word from the woman whose son wants to learn the violin. She found

Pa's terms "perfectly acceptable" and will bring her son for his first lesson next week. Hooray!

September 12, 1865

Tonight we see *King Lear*. I have not been able to finish reading the play, so I do not know how it turns out. But I must confess that, so far, I cannot understand why Jed thinks William Shakespeare is such a great writer.

September 13, 1865

I have an announcement to make: *King Lear* is a wonderful play! It made a great deal more sense when I saw it acted out onstage last night. I had no idea how truly sad it was! One of the king's daughters, Cordelia, has trouble saying how much she loves him, and he turns against her. The other daughters take over the kingdom and throw King Lear out of his castle.

In the end, when King Lear loses his mind, Cordelia is the only one who comforts him. But then she is killed, and he is all alone. When King Lear loses Cordelia, it is one of the saddest things I have ever seen.

When we came home, Pa was still awake, planning a first lesson for his new student. I rushed to him and threw my arms around him. He seemed startled, but he put down his fiddle and held me for a long time.

September 14, 1865

I told Jed I would like to see more plays by Shakespeare. Again, he said he would "keep his eye out" for something I might enjoy.

September 19, 1865

Pa had the first lesson with his new music student today. He is a boy about eight years old. He came with his mother, who introduced herself as Mrs. Charles Edmonds and her son as Master Charles Edmonds Jr.

Mrs. Edmonds said that Charles's violin had belonged to her husband, who had been killed in the war. Pa said he was terribly sorry and that he would be honored to help Charles learn to play.

Jane Ellen and I took Baby Abe to Pa's room. When he was settled, I peeked through the door and watched Pa teach Charles Edmonds Jr. how to play the violin.

First, he helped Charles hold the violin properly under his chin. Then he showed him how to grasp the bow and draw it across the strings.

At first, Charles could make no sound at all, but Pa was very patient. He put his arms around Charles and made little adjustments to the way the boy was moving the bow.

Eventually Charles began to make sounds. At first they were scratching sounds. Then they were screeching sounds. Still, Pa was patient.

Finally, Charles took a deep breath. With Pa guiding his hand, he drew the bow slowly and steadily across the strings. The sound was low and rich and sweet. It hung in the air for a moment, then died away slowly.

Pa looked happier than I have seen him in months. "Yes! Yes!" he shouted. "Good boy! Excellent!"

Charles was so excited he almost dropped the violin. When I looked at Mrs. Edmonds, there were tears on her cheeks.

September 22, 1865

At breakfast, I asked Jed if his eye was still out for more plays we could see. He laughed and said he would find something soon.

Meanwhile, Jane Ellen is helping me read *Romeo and Juliet*.

September 26, 1865

Charles Edmonds had his second violin lesson with Pa today. After the lesson, Mrs. Edmonds told Pa how pleased she was with his teaching. She said it meant the world to her to hear the sound of her husband's violin again.

Pa just smiled and nodded. He actually seemed a bit shy.

September 27, 1865

I am finding *Romeo and Juliet* a bit easier to understand than *King Lear*. The story is very sweet. And Juliet is so young! Jane Ellen says she is only a few years older than I.

September 28, 1865

Today I went with Pa on his rounds of the theatres. None of them need more musicians, but people tell him to keep checking.

I thought Pa would be discouraged, but he did not seem so at all. On the way home, he talked a great deal about Charles Edmonds and his mother, and how happy he was to have such a good student.

September 29, 1865

Jane Ellen got another letter from Becky Lee in Gettysburg. Becky Lee says times there are very hard, for whites and Negroes alike. Many freed slaves have moved north. There is not enough work. Jed says times are hard all over the country.

October 3, 1865

I have finished *Romeo and Juliet*. It ends terribly sadly, just like *King Lear*! Romeo and Juliet both die! Did Mr. Shakespeare write no plays in which everything turns out all right?

October 6, 1865

I am still worried that we will become poor. Pa had two more inquiries about music lessons this week, but that is all. I know Jed does not earn very much money from his newspaper writing. Jane Ellen cannot tutor children because of Baby Abe and her fragile health.

If Pa does not find more work soon, I worry that we will not be able to pay our rent.

October 9, 1865

I have started reading another play by Shakespeare. It is called *A Midsummer Night's Dream.* Jane Ellen has assured me that this one ends happily.

October 11, 1865

I have a job! A wonderful job at the Olympic Theatre!

Here is how it happened. Today Pa again took me with him on his rounds. We went first to Niblo's Garden Theatre, then to Wallack's Theatre. At both these theatres, the doormen were very rude and said their theatres still did not need any musicians. Then we went to the Olympic, where Mrs. John Wood is starring in *Pocahontas*.

The matinee show had just finished and people were streaming out of the theatre. We waited until the crowd cleared, then Pa asked to speak with the stage manager.

The stage manager was very polite, but said they did not need any musicians. He said the only job they had available was for a girl to help dress Mrs. Wood in her costumes for the next play, which opens tomorrow.

I spoke up immediately. I said I was very interested in the theatre and would love a job dressing Mrs. Wood. Before Pa could say anything, the stage manager asked me how old I was — and I did a dreadful thing. I lied about my age! Instead of telling him I was eleven, I said I was thirteen! Pa looked at me but still didn't speak. I think he was too shocked.

The stage manager asked if I had had any experience in the theatre. I told him I was currently studying all the plays of Shakespeare. I said I liked *Romeo and Juliet*, but *King Lear* was my favorite. I said I thought Shakespeare was an excellent writer.

The stage manager laughed and told Pa to bring me back at six o'clock to meet Mrs. Wood.

All the way home, I begged Pa to let me take the job. At first he said absolutely not, that the theatre was no place for a young girl. I reminded him that he had met my mother when she attended a theatre in Richmond and saw him play his violin onstage.

I told him working in the theatre was much

better than working in the factories, where hundreds and hundreds of young girls work.

I told him it was a perfect job for me because most days I could still stay home and help Jane Ellen with Baby Abe.

I told him it was even more perfect because I really *am* interested in the theatre.

Before I could tell him anything else, he said I could accept the job.

Later

I have met Mrs. Wood. She is plump, proud, and very outgoing. She is not only the leading actress in the company — she is the manager of the whole theatre!

I will work backstage, helping Mrs. Wood and the other actresses get dressed for their roles in a play called *The Streets of New York*.

She says I will not see much of the play, as all my work will be "behind the scenes." But I do not care! I will be working in the theatre! And I will earn five dollars a week!

October 12, 1865

I have had my first night as a dresser. The work is a bit more difficult than I had imagined. There are many costume changes, and little time to make them between scenes in the play.

It was also a bit of a chore fitting Mrs. Wood into her costumes. She kept whispering, "Hurry! Hurry!" as I struggled to fasten the tiny silver buttons on her dresses.

October 14, 1865

Late. Home. Can't write. Too tired.

October 15, 1865

There are no performances of *The Streets of New York* today because it is Sunday. Thank goodness! I am afraid I have fallen a little behind in my lessons with Jane Ellen. I will try to use today to catch up.

October 17, 1865

My work at the theatre is still difficult but getting smoother. All the actresses are now arriving onstage in time for their scenes, with nearly all their costume pieces in place. I fear I am still behind in my schoolwork, however.

As I write this, I can hear Pa teaching Charles Edmonds in the front room. Mrs. Edmonds is watching the lesson, as she always does. Charles seems to be getting better.

Pa once tried to teach me to play the violin, but was not successful. He was patient, but I am afraid I was not.

October 20, 1865

As Pa walked me home from the theatre last night, he talked about what a good student Charles Edmonds is. Pa knows I am a little behind in my lessons with Jane Ellen.

He told me that Charles is applying himself. "And that," Pa said, "is the secret of learning."

For goodness sakes, Pa! I intend to apply myself! I am just too busy and tired these days.

October 21, 1865

It is late at night. I have just finished another week at the Olympic Theatre. My fingers are red and sore from hundreds of buttonings and unbuttonings. My back aches from carrying dresses, coats, corsets, hats, shoes, boots, and scarves to and from the costume shop. I am very, very, very, very tired. But I am also very, very, very, very happy.

Mrs. Wood says I am doing "a fine job." She is not one to give compliments, so her words make me very proud. And I *love* working "behind the scenes." I can hear the whole play, and see some of it when I am not hurrying to get the actresses ready to go onstage.

I am beginning to think I might like a career in the theatre.

October 22, 1865

A beautiful autumn Sunday. Our whole family went on an outing this afternoon, even Jane Ellen and Baby Abe! They both seem much healthier now that the weather has grown cooler.

Jed took us to Central Park. The park is filled with lakes, lawns, bridges, and roads — and so many people! Men walked about in their war uniforms. Women wore shawls and hats or kerchiefs. There were many small children being pushed about in strollers.

The leaves were changing, and the park was filled with beautiful reds, oranges, and yellows. It was like a piece of open country in the middle of the city.

I must confess that when we got home, I was a little bit homesick. We did not have to go to a park to see leaves change in Gettysburg.

October 24, 1865

Tuesdays have become busy, noisy days in our home. Pa now has four students. The sounds in the parlor are sometimes truly terrible! But Pa seems very happy teaching. He says Charles Edmonds has the most natural ability of the four.

Natural ability. I wonder what my natural ability is?

October 28, 1865

Last night as I was helping Mrs. Wood get dressed, I asked how she had come to be the manager of her own theatre. She said she had simply gotten tired of always waiting for someone else to hire her to perform. Now she hires herself!

November 6, 1865

This is the last week *The Streets of New York* will play at the theatre. A new play called *The*

Sleeping Beauty in the Wood opens this Saturday. No one has said anything to me about staying on as a dresser for that play. I am worried that I will be without a job again soon.

November 8, 1865

Tonight when I was squeezing Mrs. Wood into her corset, I built up my courage and asked her what would happen when *The Sleeping Beauty in the Wood* came into the theatre. At first, she didn't seem to understand what I meant. When I told her I was worried about my job, she seemed quite surprised.

She said that I was a wonderful dresser, and of course she wants me to stay on and help the actresses in the new play! When Pa arrived to walk me home, I was floating on air.

November 11, 1865

The Sleeping Beauty in the Wood opened tonight. Things did not go smoothly.

There are many, many costume changes, and I am embarrassed to admit that not everyone arrived onstage fully dressed. Several actors forgot what they were supposed to say. Mr. Ponisi, the prompter, had to call out their lines in a loud whisper from offstage.

Still, the audience seemed to enjoy the show. I suspect most had no idea what was going on behind the scenes.

November 15, 1865

This morning, Jed and I had a discussion about plays. I said I thought *The Sleeping Beauty in the Wood* was silly and scant — probably because it is meant mostly for children — and that *The Streets of New York* was a bit overdone: The good people were too good, and the bad people were too bad. I told him that in my opinion, nothing I had seen at the Olympic Theatre came close to the writing of Mr. Shakespeare.

Jed laughed and said perhaps I should write his articles for the newspaper.

I know he was teasing, but I think I might actually enjoy that job.

November 20, 1865

Mrs. Edmonds stayed for tea after Charles's lesson this afternoon. Pa sent me to the market on the corner to fetch some cream and asked that I takes Charles with me.

On the way to the store, I asked Charles about his father. Charles said he was a lieutenant with a New York cavalry regiment. He was shot in the Battle of Williamsburg and died of blood poisoning in a field hospital.

Charles has a slight stammer. But he speaks very earnestly and seems to remember his father with much love. "It was a terrible, terrible tragedy," he said. I wanted to hug his skinny little body and comfort him.

When we got home, Pa and Mrs. Edmonds were sitting together on the settee in the parlor. I could tell that Mrs. Edmonds had been crying. I cannot say for sure, but I suspect she had been talking about Charles's father, too.

November 22, 1865

The Sleeping Beauty in the Wood has been playing for over a week now, and several of the actors still do not know their lines!

Mr. Ponisi has gotten quite cross about the situation. Tonight he was nearly shouting the lines to the actors from offstage!

November 28, 1865

Our lives are much more orderly these days. Pa now has seven students. I am doing much better with my lessons with Jane Ellen. We finished *A Midsummer Night's Dream*, and now I am reading *As You Like It*.

December 4, 1865

I heard some exciting news at the theatre today. John Wilkes Booth's brother Edwin Booth is returning to the stage! People have convinced him that he should not have to pay for the crimes of his brother by giving up his career as an actor. So in January he will perform *Hamlet* by William Shakespeare at the Winter Garden Theatre.

Mrs. Wood says that Shakespeare is the greatest writer who ever lived, that *Hamlet* is the greatest play ever written, and that Edwin Booth is the greatest actor of our time.

I think I *must* find a way to see Edwin Booth in this play!

December 5, 1865

I asked Jed about going to see Mr. Edwin Booth play *Hamlet*. He said he would inquire at his newspaper about tickets.

December 9, 1865

Another show is opening at the theatre next week. Mrs. Wood asked if I could please come in early tomorrow to help organize the new costumes. I guess I am now an official dresser at the Olympic Theatre!

December 11, 1865

I asked Jed if he had had any success getting tickets for Edwin Booth's *Hamlet*. He said it had slipped his mind! I asked him to please try to remember, as everyone at the theatre is talking about this event.

December 14, 1865

I have saved enough from my wages to buy Christmas presents for everyone. I am giving Pa a pair of gloves; Jed, a new pen; Jane Ellen, a red scarf; and Baby Abe, a rag doll.

December 20, 1865

I asked Jed again about seeing *Hamlet*. He said many people wanted to see the play, and it is extremely difficult to get tickets. I asked him to please, please keep trying.

December 23, 1865

Jane Ellen and I went shopping for our Christmas dinner today at Washington Market. I have never seen anything like it!

Every day, farmers bring their produce from the countryside to the market. Hundreds of beef carcasses hang from hooks in the ceiling. Butcher counters are piled high with ducks, turkeys, and chickens. Women carry baskets filled with breads, pastries, and muffins.

There seems to be much more food in the land since the war has ended.

December 24, 1865
Christmas Eve

We awoke this morning to a blanket of snow all over the city. I was delighted — I thought we were surely going to enjoy a beautifully white Christmas.

The beauty lasted only a short while, though, for soon it began to rain. The cold rain washed away the snow, and now our street looks dirty and bleak again. I fear our first Christmas in New York will be a bit dreary.

December 25, 1865
Christmas Day

I was wrong. Our first New York Christmas will not be dreary at all. We awoke to a beautiful Christmas morning. It is like a soft, spring day in the middle of winter. Pa said it is our Christmas gift from the Lord.

Later

I am happier than I can say. I have been given a priceless treasure.

This evening, when it came time to open our Christmas gifts, Jed and Jane Ellen handed me a big box wrapped in green paper.

Everyone watched as I opened the box. Inside, I found a great nest of crumpled newspaper. Buried in the newspaper was a brown envelope.

I opened the envelope and pulled out a small slip of paper.

I stared at the slip of paper for a long moment before I realized what it was: a ticket to the Winter Garden Theatre for the evening of January 3. That is the night Edwin Booth returns to the stage in *Hamlet*!

I am going to see *Hamlet*! Hooray! Hooray!

December 26, 1865

Tonight I asked Mrs. Wood if I might be excused from my duties as a dresser to see Edwin Booth perform *Hamlet* next week. I told her my brother had given me a ticket as a Christmas gift.

Mrs. Wood said my brother must be a very important person, as tickets are almost impossible to get! She said that for such a special event, she would certainly arrange for someone to cover my duties backstage.

January 1, 1866
New Year's Day

Pa got dressed in his best clothes today. I asked if he had a job. He said, "No, I am just going calling."

Pa going calling?

January 2, 1866

There was a very unkind article in one of the papers today about Mr. Edwin Booth. The writer thought that rather than playing in *Hamlet*, he should play in *Julius Caesar* — as the person who murders Caesar!

This is mean and unkind. Mr. Booth never supported the South and even retired from acting when the President was assassinated. I hope he is not booed when he appears onstage tomorrow night.

January 3, 1866

Tonight I will finally wear my lacy yellow dress. I had been saving it for a special occasion. Jane Ellen and I spent much of the day working on it. I have grown so much taller in the past nine months that we had to let out what we had taken up last spring!

Later

Jed and I are at the Winter Garden Theatre. Hundreds of people are crowding to get inside. Women are wearing gold powdered wigs and jewels. Men are in their finest coats and hats. This is clearly a great occasion. We must hurry now to get to our seats.

Later

I am finally settled in my seat. But I must put away my writing now, as the play is about to begin.

Later

It is near midnight. I am home. I have had an astonishing experience. I will try to write about it tomorrow.

January 4, 1866

I will now try to describe what happened last night.

I saw Mr. Edwin Booth perform *Hamlet* at the Winter Garden Theatre. He was not booed. In fact, people cheered and cheered when he appeared onstage. They waved handkerchiefs and threw bouquets of flowers.

Mr. Booth took a deep, deep bow. When he stood up, there were tears in his eyes. Then he went on to perform the play.

There was an entire castle onstage. There was a ghost, and soldiers, and much fighting with swords. And in the center of it all was Mr. Edwin Booth.

Mr. Booth did not shout or wave his arms as many of the players did. And even though he sometimes spoke the poetry of Shakespeare very softly, I understood every word.

I was so sad when he was killed that I cried and cried. But when he came out for his curtain call, I wept for joy that he was not really dead.

I wish life could be like that.

January 6, 1866

I have been reading *Hamlet* in Jed's Shakespeare book. As I read it, I see and hear Mr. Edwin Booth, over and over.

January 8, 1866

I am weeping again. I just read the words spoken over Hamlet when he dies.

"Goodnight Sweet Prince, and flights of angels sing thee to thy rest." Isn't that beautiful?

January 9, 1866

This morning, I talked with Jed about why Mr. Edwin Booth is such a great actor. I reminded him that when President Lincoln gave his speech at Gettysburg, a magazine said he had spoken "from the heart to the heart."

That is what I believe Mr. Edwin Booth does onstage. When he performed *Hamlet*, I felt I always knew exactly what he was thinking and feeling. He spoke directly from his heart to mine.

January 10, 1866

I think I am in love with Mr. Edwin Booth. I cannot stop thinking about how he looked in his black costume, and how he walked, and how he spoke. He is surely the greatest actor who has ever lived.

January 13, 1866

There was an engraving of Edwin Booth on the cover of *Harper's Weekly* newspaper today. He has dark, wavy hair, sad eyes, and a strong nose. He looks very thoughtful. I wonder, I wonder what he is thinking about.

January 15, 1866

I have noticed that Mrs. Edmonds is staying longer and longer after Charles's lessons. Today she and Pa sat together in the parlor for almost an hour.

After she left, Pa went to his room and played his violin until Jane Ellen called him to supper. His music was joyful and spirited.

Could Pa's feelings about Mrs. Charles Edmonds be like mine for Mr. Edwin Booth?

January 18, 1866

I spoke to Jane Ellen about Pa and Mrs. Edmonds. She thinks it is good for Pa to have a lady friend. She said he must be very lonely. I told her he shouldn't be lonely, that our house is filled with people. She said there were many ways to be lonely.

January 20, 1866

I have been thinking about Pa's loneliness. Perhaps Jane Ellen is right. I myself have sometimes felt very lonely, even in our crowded little home.

I am sure Edwin Booth has felt terrible loneliness in his life. I can tell from the sadness in his eyes.

January 23, 1866

I have done a bold thing. I have written a letter to Mr. Edwin Booth. Here is what I said:

Dear Mr. Booth,

I had the wonderful pleasure of seeing you perform *Hamlet* at the Winter Garden Theatre on January 3. I feel your performance changed my life.

I am concerned that you might be feeling lonely and sad. I heard that you had retired from acting because of your brother John. I am very glad you changed your mind. I believe President Lincoln would be glad, too.

If you would like to correspond with someone who understands your loneliness, I would very much like to hear from you.

Yours most sincerely,

Virginia Dickens

January 28, 1866

It has been nearly a week since I wrote to Mr. Booth. I still have not received a reply. But I know he is very busy.

January 30, 1866

Last night Pa played at a very fancy charity ball for the Nursery and Children's Hospital. Mrs. Edmonds had helped to organize the event. The conductor of the orchestra was an acquaintance of hers, and last week she arranged for Pa to play his violin for him.

The conductor said Pa is very talented and hired him on the spot. He even said he might have more jobs for Pa in the future.

Mrs. Edmonds and Charles went to hear Pa play at the ball. Afterward, they all went out for ice cream! I will admit I was a bit jealous when Pa told me this. But when I thought about Pa's loneliness, I calmed down.

I wonder: Are Mrs. Edmonds and Charles lonely, too?

February 5, 1866

Another play opened in the theatre today. It is called *A New Way to Pay Old Debts*. There are only five actresses, so I will not have to work nearly as hard getting everyone dressed.

February 6, 1866

Today when Mrs. Edmonds was here with Charles for his lesson, she spoke very sweetly to me. She said, "Your father always says such nice things about you, Ginny. I hope we can get to know each other better."

I wonder when Pa says these nice things. Does he call on Mrs. Edmonds a lot?

February 7, 1866

Pa is growing a beard! At first I thought he had just forgotten to shave for a few days. But when I asked him about it, he said he had been the only man in the charity ball orchestra who did not have whiskers. He thinks the beard might bring him luck.

I think he will look very handsome. But I will miss seeing the dimple in his chin.

February 11, 1866

Nearly three weeks, and still no answer from Mr. Booth. He must get many letters from people who admire his talent. I imagine it takes him quite a while to answer them all.

February 12, 1866

Today is President Lincoln's birthday. He would have been fifty-six years old today.

I once read that President Lincoln grew his beard because a little girl told him he would look more handsome if he had a beard.

I wonder if Mrs. Charles Edmonds has anything to do with Pa's whiskers.

February 16, 1866

Wonderful news! Today Pa was offered a regular job with the orchestra that played at the charity ball! Perhaps his beard has indeed brought him luck.

February 22, 1866

An amazing thing has happened. I am so excited I can barely write. It is the most wonderful thing that has happened to me in all my life.

Tonight I am to have a part onstage! I shall perform the role of Waiting Woman in the play *A New Way to Pay Old Debts*.

Here is how this came about:

When I arrived at the theatre tonight, I learned that the actress who normally plays Waiting Woman had come down with a terrible case of laryngitis. She cannot speak above a whisper.

The Waiting Woman actress is very close to my height and size. When I heard about the situation, I spoke right up. I told Mrs. Wood that the Waiting Woman costume fit me perfectly and that I was sure I could perform the role! The play closes in less than a week, and Mrs. Wood does not want to hire another actress for only a few performances. So she agreed!

I shall have only three lines, but Mrs. Wood says they are very important to the play and I must speak them loudly and clearly.

Here is what I am to say:

"Foh, what a smell is here!"

Then: "I begin to feel faint!"

And finally: "Sweet madam, keep your glove to your nose!"

Later

I am dressed in my Waiting Woman costume. I was very confident when I spoke to Mrs. Wood, but now I feel my confidence is leaving me. I wish Mr. Booth were here to give me advice!

Later

In less than an hour, I will be onstage. I keep saying my three lines over and over and over. Mr. Ponisi has told me not to worry, that he will be there to call out my lines if I forget. That would be so embarrassing! I pray, I pray that I do not forget my lines.

Later

I am terrified. I have never been so frightened. I thought writing in my journal might calm me, but it has not. My hand is shaking so badly I fear I will never be able to read what I am writing now.

I tell myself that there is nothing to be afraid of, but my heart will not stop pounding.

I must go now and stand in the wings and listen for Frank Wellborn to shout: "Ah!

Better and better!" That is Waiting Woman's cue to go onstage.

Later

It is over. I am home.

My time onstage seemed to fly by. When I came off, I could not be certain I had spoken *any* of my lines. But Mr. Ponisi assured me I had spoken them all, and had done a fine job!

I am the happiest I have ever been. When Pa came to walk me home, Mrs. Wood told him I had the makings of a real actress!

When we got back, Jed, Jane Ellen, and Baby Abe were all asleep. But I insisted on waking Jed to tell him my news.

February 23, 1866

Tonight I shall have my second performance as Waiting Woman. I feel a bit calmer, but not much.

I know Mr. Booth has played the part of Hamlet many times. I wonder: Is he also nervous before he steps onto the stage? I think I shall write to him and ask him.

Later

I have completed my second performance as Waiting Woman. I was not shaking so badly, and I believe I said my lines more clearly.

As I was leaving the theatre, the actress who normally plays the part whispered that I had done a good job. It is clear her voice will not return in time for her to perform again before the show closes. I tried to feel sorry for her, but I am afraid I was too happy for myself.

February 24, 1866

Tonight is my final performance as Waiting Woman. Pa, Jed, Jane Ellen, Baby Abe, Mrs. Edmonds, and Charles are all coming to see me perform.

Last night, when I said the line "I begin to feel faint," I pretended to swoon a little. The audience laughed. I think I shall try swooning a bit more tonight.

Later

Just before I went onstage, Mr. Ponisi told me not to swoon when I said I felt faint. Still, I think tonight was my best performance yet.

After the show, everyone met me backstage. Pa clapped and whistled when he saw me. Jed said I had done a very respectable job and that he was proud of me. Jane Ellen wanted to know if I had had any trouble memorizing my lines. Charles said he thought I was funny.

But Mrs. Edmonds said the nicest thing of all. She put her arms around me and whispered that I was absolutely radiant.

February 25, 1866

I have spent all this Sunday afternoon thinking of different ways I might have said my Waiting Woman lines. I believe with a little more practice, I could have been even better!

I am already wondering what roles I might play in the future. A new show opens tomorrow night: *The Count of Monte Cristo*.

Unfortunately, there do not seem to be any roles for women my height and size.

February 26, 1866

Pa told me this morning that I did not need to work as a dresser any more. He is proud to be able to support us all now, I think, and wants me to spend more time on my lessons. But I told him that I do not want to quit my job. I love the theatre — even if I have to work behind the scenes for now.

So tonight I will go back to being a dresser, until I am given another opportunity to go on the stage.

February 27, 1866

Guess what? Now Jed is growing a beard, too! But Jed's beard has never been good. It is wispy and thin and patchy — not thick like Pa's or President Lincoln's. Jane Ellen hates it!

February 28, 1866

We have all been teasing Jed about his beard. Today I found this notice in the paper:

WHISKERS AND MUSTACHES!

One Dollar! Dr. Briggs's Grecian Compound is guaranteed to grow a beautiful set of whiskers on the smoothest face in five weeks. This wonderful discovery has been used by the elite of both Paris and London. Entire satisfaction given or money cheerfully refunded.

I clipped the advertisement from the newspaper and left it on Jed's dresser.

March 1, 1866

I have been reading the plays of Shakespeare, thinking of roles I might perform. I believe I should most enjoy playing Juliet.

This morning, I stood in front of the mirror and practiced saying Juliet's lines: "O Romeo, Romeo! Wherefore art thou Romeo?"

March 2, 1866

It is very late. I cannot sleep. That is because I cannot stop crying.

As I was laying out costumes tonight, I overheard a conversation. The actor who played Frank Wellborn was talking to Mr. Ponisi about my performance as Waiting Woman.

This is what I heard him say:

"Our young Miss Dickens was quite good, didn't you think?"

And this is what I heard Mr. Ponisi reply: "Yes. It's a shame she's so plain."

March 3, 1866

I did not go to my job at the theatre today. I pretended to be sick.

Until yesterday, I had never even thought about whether I was plain or pretty. Now I know the answer without ever asking the question.

March 4, 1866

"It's a shame she's so plain."

I keep hearing those words over and over. Was my mother plain? I pulled out my locket today and looked at her picture.

She was indeed *not* plain, with her soft curls and sweet smile. What happened to me?

Later

I have written another letter to Edwin Booth. This is what I said:

Dear Mr. Booth,

I know you have not responded to my previous letters because of your busy schedule. But now I have a question of utmost importance.

Here it is: Must a girl be pretty to be an actress?

The girl who played Ophelia in your production of *Hamlet* was quite pretty indeed. It is difficult to tell if Mrs. Wood was pretty when she was younger, but I suspect she might have been.

I am not pretty. I am plain. Do you believe I can still have a career in the theatre?

I eagerly await your reply.

Virginia Dickens

March 5, 1866

I returned to my job as a dresser tonight. I did not speak to Mr. Ponisi. When he said, "Sorry you were sick yesterday," I just nodded and quickly moved away from him.

March 6, 1866

I do not know what to do. Mr. Ponisi's hateful words will not leave my mind. I wish Mr. Booth would reply to my letter.

March 7, 1866

Tonight, Jane Ellen knocked on my door. She asked why I have been so moody.

I had not intended to share my shame with anyone. But I could not stop my sorrow over Mr. Ponisi's words from bubbling forth. I even told Jane Ellen about my most recent letter to Edwin Booth.

Jane Ellen was furious! She said Mr. Ponisi must think a girl is pretty only if she curls her hair and paints her face and wears a tight corset! She said that my beauty was simple and natural, the sort that old fools like Mr. Ponisi are too blind and stupid to see!

I imagine Jane Ellen was only saying all this to make me feel better. Still, I am grateful for her outrage.

March 10, 1866

My work at the theatre has not felt the same since I overheard Mr. Ponisi talking about me. I wonder if perhaps I should quit soon.

March 12, 1866

Today I received this letter:

Dear Virginia,

First, let me apologize for not answering your letters sooner. As you can imagine, my schedule is quite exhausting.

Now let me address your pressing question. You must not be concerned with your physical beauty. There is beauty in speech, in movement, and in language that far transcends mere "prettiness." That is the beauty you must always look for in your art.

You seem to have talents well beyond your skills as an actress. Indeed, it seems from your letters that you are already an excellent writer.

Remember that we still speak of William Shakespeare with reverence and respect, while the actors of his day are all forgotten.

You say that my performance speaks from the heart to the heart. That is a wonderful compliment. It is also the advice I would give to you. Always strive to speak from your heart directly to the hearts of others, and you will succeed — in whatever career you choose.

The letter was signed "Yours Sincerely, Mr. Edwin Booth."

I will treasure this letter always — but not because it came from Mr. Edwin Booth. In fact, Mr. Booth did not write this letter.

How do I know? Because in my letters to Mr. Booth, I never mentioned that I thought he spoke from the heart to the heart.

I told that to only Jed.

March 13, 1866

I have decided never to tell Jed that I know he wrote the letter. But his words have stayed with me, especially these: "You are already an excellent writer."

Jed's opinion of my writing means everything to me. But in the days before I received the letter, I am afraid I would have quickly traded being a good writer for being a pretty actress.

That would have been a terrible mistake. I love finding ways to say what I truly think and feel. And what I truly think and feel right now is that I would rather be a good writer than anything else on earth.

March 14, 1866

Tonight, during the play, when everything was busy and hectic, I decided to quit my job as a dresser. I want to read, and study harder with Jane Ellen, and go to a real school next fall.

I was suddenly so clear about this that as soon as the show was over, I told Mrs. Wood I would be leaving after this week. I told her I needed more time to spend on my schoolwork.

"I understand perfectly," she said. "But should you ever wish to return to the theatre, you will always be welcome here."

I *will* return to the theatre someday, but not as a dresser. I will be like Mrs. Wood. She became a theatre manager so she could hire herself. I will write a play so I can hire myself! And I will give myself the best part. The part will be a girl who some people think is plain. But, in fact, she is not. She is simple and natural, and she is an excellent writer.

March 15, 1866

This morning at breakfast, I announced that I was leaving my job at the theatre. I said I wanted to work harder on my lessons, and asked if we could discuss my schooling for next year. Everyone seemed pleased with my decision. And Pa assured me that next year we would find the best school in New York for me.

March 16, 1866

At supper tonight, Jed talked about a speech President Johnson gave that has angered many people. In the speech, President

Johnson called the congressmen who do not agree with him "traitors." Jed said he thought that such behavior was shameful. Then he turned to me and asked what I thought.

I said I had to wonder what President Lincoln would think of President Johnson's speech. I reminded him how President Lincoln had called upon the "better angels of our nature." I said I did not think President Johnson was calling upon the better angels of *his* nature when he called the senators names.

Later, when I got home from the theatre, Jed asked my permission to use my thoughts about Lincoln and Johnson in an article he is writing for the newspaper. I told him I would be pleased for him to use my ideas.

In fact, I am more than pleased. I am bursting with pride.

March 17, 1866

Today was my last day at the Olympic Theatre. Between the matinee and the evening shows, I took a walk with Charles Edmonds.

On our walk, we passed an organ grinder. He had a little monkey and, after every song, the monkey would take off his hat and scamper amongst the crowd, collecting pennies.

Charles laughed so hard that I thought he would fall over. Charles has a soft heart for animals. He told me he likes all kinds — "monkeys, bears, giraffes, penguins, pelicans, and ostriches, just to name a few" — he said.

I told Charles that I want to be a writer someday. He told me that he wants to be an animal doctor and play the violin.

March 18, 1866

"Lately in my prayers, I have been talking with Elizabeth. I truly believe she will not mind if I marry again."

Those were Pa's opening words when he called us into the front room tonight.

Pa went on to say that he believes my mother requires only that he marry a good woman who will be kind to him and me and Jed. He then told us that he has found such a person. "She is Mrs. Charles Edmonds," he said. "And today I asked her to be my wife."

Jane Ellen wiped tears of joy from her eyes. She said that Mrs. Edmonds was a fine woman. Jed hugged Pa and congratulated him. Baby Abe giggled as if he were happy, too.

I couldn't stop smiling. It's strange, but I believe I was happiest for Charles Edmonds. I think that little boy deserves a father like Pa.

March 20, 1866

Tonight we are going to celebrate Pa and Mrs. Edmonds's engagement. I am preparing a funny joke to play on everyone.

Later

We had a wonderful party. Everyone seemed a bit awkward at first — until I played my joke.

While Jane Ellen and Mrs. Edmonds were setting the table and Pa and Jed and Charles were staring at the walls, I snuck into Baby Abe's room. I quickly drew a beard and mustache on his little face. Then I called frantically for everyone to come see "the miracle!"

Everyone ran into the room. For a minute, they all just stared at Baby Abe. "He must have ordered Dr. Briggs's Grecian Compound!" I said. Then Baby Abe grinned, and we all burst out laughing. I have never seen Pa laugh so hard. Jed and Jane Ellen laughed hard, too. Mrs. Edmonds and Charles looked puzzled at first, but then they joined in.

Later, after supper, Pa brought out his fiddle. Jane Ellen played the piano. Jed danced with Mrs. Edmonds, and I danced with Charles. Even Baby Abe danced — he held on to a chair and pumped his little legs to the beat of the music.

As I looked around the room crowded with people, I had an amazing thought. Less than three years ago, when Pa and Jed were missing outside Gettysburg, our family seemed to be made up of just one person — me. Then Pa and Jed came back, and we were three again. Then Jed married Jane Ellen, and we were four. Then Baby Abe was born, and we were five. Now Mrs. Edmonds and Charles will join us, and we will be seven.

The Bible says for everything there is a season:

A time to kill, and a time to heal.
A time to break down, and a time to build up.
A time to weep, and a time to laugh.
A time to mourn, and a time to dance.

Tonight was our time to dance.

Life in America
in 1865

Historical Note

When the Civil War ended on April 8, 1865, many people hoped that President Abraham Lincoln could lead the nation through the difficult period of healing with the same wisdom and compassion he had shown throughout the war. Those hopes were shattered when Lincoln was assassinated by the actor John Wilkes Booth at Ford's Theatre on April 14.

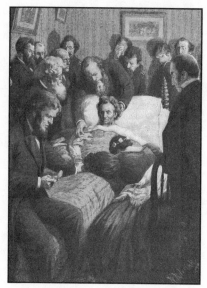

President Lincoln's bedside

The task of rebuilding the nation fell to Lincoln's successor, Andrew Johnson. During the war, when he was vice president, Johnson had often called for harsh treatment of the South and its leaders. But as President, Johnson favored much more lenient treatment of the formerly Confederate states.

President Andrew Johnson

Many Northerners believed Johnson's Reconstruction plan was too generous to the South. The differences of opinion led to bitter battles in Congress. The disagreements eventually led Congress to call for Johnson's impeachment in 1868. He retained his presidency by only one vote.

At the end of the Civil War, New York City was a crowded, colorful world. The richest city in the country, it was home to many wealthy

A view of New York City in 1865

merchants, bankers, and politicians. But its poor neighborhoods were crowded with immigrant families living and working in terrible conditions. For rich and poor alike, attending the theater was a popular source of entertainment — and escape.

Edwin Booth is considered one of America's greatest Shakespearean actors. At the time his brother, John Wilkes Booth, assassinated Abraham Lincoln, Edwin Booth's fame was well established. The fallout from this terrible act forced Edwin to temporarily retire. Less than a year later, he returned to the stage in the role of Hamlet. Many people feared that the public would reject him and he would be booed off the stage.

This was not the case. Here's how one newspaper described the audience's reaction to Edwin Booth's first appearance in the play: "The men stamped, clapped their hands, and hurrahed, continuously; the ladies rose in their seats and waved a thousand handkerchiefs; and

for full five minutes a scene of wild excitement forbade the progress of the play." Clearly, the New York audience did not hold Edwin Booth responsible for his brother's crime.

Actor Edwin Booth

About the Authors

Mary Pope Osborne and Will Osborne say, "Because of Will's career, we've been involved in the theater together for many years. It was wonderful to collaborate on *A Time to Dance* and explore the world of New York theater in the 1860s. We loved putting Ginny into that world and imagining her thrill at going onstage for the first time."

Mary Pope Osborne is the award-winning author of many books for children, including the best-selling Magic Tree House series; *Adaline Falling Star*; the My America books, *My Brother's Keeper* and *After the Rain*; and two

Dear America books, *Standing in the Light* and *My Secret War*.

Will Osborne has worked in the professional theater for many years as an actor, director, and playwright. He and Mary have collaborated on eleven books for young readers, including *Jason and the Argonauts*, *The Deadly Power of Medusa*, and the Magic Tree House Research Guides series.

Mary and Will divide their time between New York City and Goshen, Connecticut, with their Norfolk terrier, Bailey.

Acknowledgments

The authors would like to thank their editor, Amy Griffin, for her wonderful support and guidance, and Lisa Sandell for her assistance. They would also like to thank Dr. Jack Hrkach of Ithaca College for his excellent research and advice, and the New York Historical Society for providing access to the *Spirit of the Times*, *Harper's Weekly*, and other periodicals from the time.

Grateful acknowledgment is made for permission to reprint the following:

Cover Portrait by Glenn Harrington

Page 101: President Lincoln's bedside, Culver Pictures, New York.
Page 102: President Andrew Johnson, Library of Congress, via Scholastic's Online Digital Archive.
Page 103: View of New York City, Culver Pictures, New York.
Page 104: Edwin Booth, Culver Pictures, New York.

Other books in the My America series

Corey's Underground Railroad Diaries
by Sharon Dennis Wyeth

Elizabeth's Jamestown Colony Diaries
by Patricia Hermes

Hope's Revolutionary War Diaries
by Kristiana Gregory

Joshua's Oregon Trail Diaries
by Patricia Hermes

Meg's Prairie Diaries
by Kate McMullan

Virginia's Civil War Diaries
by Mary Pope Osborne

For Cecilia deWolf

Copyright © 2003 by Mary Pope Osborne and Will Osborne

Library of Congress Cataloging-in-Publication Data
Osborne, Mary Pope. Osborne, Will.
A time to dance / by Mary Pope Osborne and Will Osborne.
p. cm. — (Virginia's Civil War diary ; bk. 3)
Summary: Virginia records the events of her life as her family moves to New York City
in the aftermath of the Civil War, and she begins to dream of a life in the theater.
ISBN 0-439-44341-5; 0-439-44343-1 (pbk.)
[1. Theater — Fiction. 2. Diaries — Fiction. 3. New York (N.Y.) — History —
1865–1898 — Fiction. 4. Reconstruction — Fiction.] I. Titles. II. Series.
PZ7.O81167 Tk 2003
[Fic] 21   2002044581
CIP   AC

10 9 8 7 6 5 4 3 2 1   03 04 05 06 07

The display type was set in Colwell Roman.
The text type was set in Goudy.
Photo research by Amla Sanghvi
Book design by Elizabeth B. Parisi
Printed in the U.S.A.   23
First edition, August 2003